MOG'S
Christmas

MOG'S
Christmas

written and illustrated by
Judith Kerr

HarperCollins *Children's Books*

For my friend
Mrs Cleghorn

Other books by Judith Kerr include:

First published in hardback in Great Britain by William Collins Sons & Co Ltd in 1976. First published in paperback in 1978.
This edition published by HarperCollins Children's Books in 2010

11

ISBN: 978-0-00-734705-6

Visit our website at www.harpercollins.co.uk

Printed and bound in China

One day Mog woke up
and nothing was right in her house.

Everybody was busy.
Debbie was busy.

Nicky was busy.

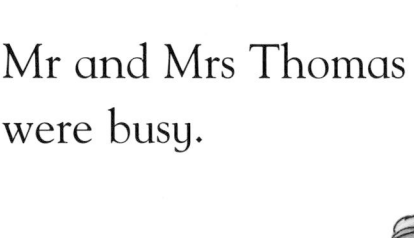

Mr and Mrs Thomas
were busy.

And there were too many people in the house.

There was a jolly uncle

...and two aunts
on tippy-toe.

Mog thought, "I don't like it here."
She went and sat outside on the window-sill.
There was nothing to do and no one to play
with, so after a while she went back to sleep.

Suddenly she woke up.
She saw something.
It was a tree.
It was a tree walking.

Mog thought, "Trees don't walk.
Trees should stay in one place.
Once trees start walking about
anything might happen."
She ran up the side of the
house in case the tree should
come and get her.
"Come down," shouted the tree.
"Come down, Mog!"
"First it walks," thought Mog,
"and now it's shouting at me.
I do not like that tree at all."
And she ran right up to the roof.

The tree went on shouting for a while.
Then it went into the house.
Mog stayed on the roof.
Some white things fell out of the sky.
Some fell on the roof and some fell
on Mog.
They were very cold.

At supper time
Mog was still on the roof.
"She must have her supper,"
said Debbie. "Mog always
has her supper."
Mrs Thomas gave Mog her supper.
But still Mog did not come down.

In the morning Mog did not come down either.
She had found a nice tall place, and she
was asleep.
She was having a lovely dream.

Mog dreamed that she was sitting on a cloud.
Some white things were falling out of the sky.
Mog tried to catch them. She was very happy.
But suddenly the cloud began to melt...

Inside the house everyone was sad
because Mog would not come down.
They were too sad to eat their breakfast.

Even the jolly uncle was sad,
and one of the aunts cried.

Suddenly there was a noise.
It was a noise in the chimney.
And then something came down it.
It came right down the chimney and
fell into the fireplace with a thump.

"It's Father Christmas!"
cried one of the aunts.
"No, dear," said the other aunt,
"Father Christmas does not
have a tail."

Debbie cried, "It's Mog!"

Mog had to have a bath.
But then...

Then everything was lovely.
The whole house was lovely.
The tree had stopped walking
about and had made itself
all pretty.

And Mog had three boiled eggs and
some turkey and a present to unwrap.

"Happy Christmas, Mog," said Debbie.